THE
BIRTH
OF
GEMINI

☼

A SHORT STORY PREQUEL TO
The Signs of the Stars

C. S. Johnson

STORY AUTHOR
C. S. Johnson

MANGA ILLUSTRATOR
Alkinz

eBook ISBN: 978-1-948464-14-7
Print ISBN: 978-1-948464-13-0

Dedicated with much love to my children, whose
smiles never fail to bring out the stars in my eyes.

This is also for Jacob, a new friend and fellow comic
book lover, and for Sam. If joy and suffering are
wisdom's teachers, you easily inspire both even after
all these years.

AUTHOR'S NOTE

Dear Reader,

Welcome once again to another one of my worlds. If you are a returning reader, you might be surprised to find another note to greet you. If you are new, this is not the usual routine; usually my notes are at the end. But I wanted to offer my welcome while giving you a warning.

This book is small and short, but it has a powerful picture of the beginning of my upcoming series, *The Signs of the Stars*, a space opera adventure I'm working on. For your enjoyment, I have included the original story itself, in written form, and also the story in manga form. I owe a great deal of thanks my illustrator, Alkinz, who worked diligently on capturing how I imagined my characters and bringing them to life, as well as my editor, Jennifer, for working with my words with her usual magic.

The Signs of the Stars was inspired by so much, including the theories of genetic memory and the question of how far people would go for home and family. This story is the introduction to Callox and Pasher, the twins who will be at the center of the series, the ones who carry the Sign of Gemini.

So, welcome to both formats, even though the story is the same. I hope you will enjoy them, and look for the official start of the series when it comes out.

Until We Meet Again,

C. S. Johnson

To Get *Awakening* (A Special Christmas Episode of
The *Starlight Chronicles*) as a bonus for picking up this
book,

Click <u>Here</u>

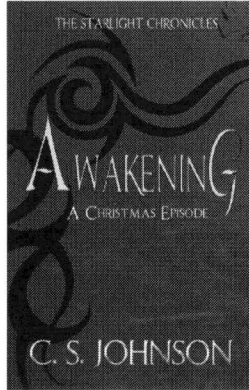

Or Download It At:
<u>https://www.csjohnson.me/awakening</u>

The Birth of Gemini

°☼°

The moment his tiny, newborn son grasped onto his forefinger, he felt the galaxy around him shift along with the vulnerability inside his heart.

The cool, steel walls of the operation room dimmed; the sounds of the medical staff in the background became muffled. His breath suddenly came in stilted, uneven gulps.

"Micheel." His wife's voice was a shaking whisper behind him.

It hardly seemed real that he was standing on the *Nebulous*, one of the many medical starships owned by Mercy Interplanetary Alliance. He had been with the company for over ten years, working faithfully port to port, planet to planet, all across the Nova Galaxy.

It hardly seemed real that he was holding his son, Callox, his hours-old, ruddy-faced offspring, whose sparse ruffle of black hair and already darkening eyes served as a reminder of his own.

Micheel felt the whisper of the still, small voice of God as it passed through his premonition.

Burning dots abruptly appeared just beneath Callox's shoulder. They twinkled in a forbidden pattern.

"Micheel … Pasher's arm … "

Micheel finally dared to look at his beloved wife. In her arms, another small, sleeping bundle glowed with identical markings.

The sign of the constellation branded on their bodies served as a marker, one indicating his twins carried the hidden code Earth's last generation had engineered into human DNA.

"It's not just Pasher, Nabelle. Callox has it, too," Micheel finally said. He traced his finger along the new constellation on Callox's shoulder, his heart filled with simultaneous fear and wonder, awed by mystic beauty and floundered by harsh reality. "The Sign of Gemini. More than appropriate, in this case."

"We need to leave. Now. Before the Collectors come," Nabelle whimpered.

"Gemini is the Sign of Order. It's not a threat."

"To my family, it is," Nabelle reminded him. "It means a change in leadership will take place. A new human order is beginning. Pasher and Callox are its forerunners. The Collectors will not let them live."

"But change is not necessarily dangerous—"

"Anyone embedded with a Sign is dangerous. That's why if the Collectors find them—"

"—they'll kill them," Micheel finished.

"They know when the Signs appear and how to track them."

"That's how they killed Esta," Micheel murmured, remembering stories of the warrior queen who bore the mark of Orion, the Sign of War, who had lived over five hundred years before.

"We will have to separate the twins," Nabelle whispered. "If we want to save them."

No. Micheel felt his breath rush out of his body. Fifteen years he had waited for his family, only to have them torn apart after barely five hours.

Before he could argue with Nabelle, the monitor by the operation room entrance beeped.

"Doctor Reshi." The familiar voice of his intern, Zara, crackled with static. "Count Lux of the Pyrian System has arrived. He has requested an audience with you."

"Lux is here? Already?" Nabelle's topaz eyes widened with sudden fear and fury. "I doubt he's here to congratulate us."

Sudden, unpleasant resolve ran through Micheel. "Rest, *ya kamar.* You just gave us our twins. Lux might be your cousin, but he doesn't know you're here."

Nabelle shuddered. "Collectors don't forget, Micheel. Why do you think he wants to see you, of all people?"

"I am a surgeon." Micheel gestured toward the robotic controls and surgical tools behind him. "Maybe he needs surgery."

"I would laugh if I wasn't so scared," Nabelle muttered.

"There's no need to be scared. I can protect us."

"How?"

Micheel pressed the button on the intercom. "Zara?"

"Yes, Doctor?"

"Tell His Grace I'm in surgery," he ordered. "I'll be with him in a few hours."

"Yes, Doctor."

"How long do you think you'll be able to get away with that?" Nabelle shuddered.

"Long enough for you and Pasher to be transported out of here."

"What?" Nabelle gaped at him.

"Here. Take these rejuvenation meds," Micheel said, placing a med patch onto her shoulder. "They'll give you a day of pain-free movement. Don't overexert yourself."

"Micheel—"

Micheel pressed another button. "Zara, I have a patient here for emergency transport," he called. "I'm sending the transport module down now."

"No!" As Nabelle struggled against him, Micheel marveled at her, at how the light subtlety of his skin colors clashed so beautifully against her bronze strength. He would miss her desperately, he knew.

"Listen," he ordered. "Once Lux is gone, I'll find a way to get Callox out of here and meet up with you." Before Nabelle could object, he held Pasher to his heart, gently kissing his baby's forehead. "I love you," he whispered. "Remember me, until we meet again."

"This is not a good plan, Micheel."

"Don't I know it." He drew her close, letting his lips hover just above hers for a long moment, before kissing her deeply. "But I can't lose my family."

The guardrails around Nabelle's bed shifted, and a small, darkened glass top came down over the bed, sealing them off.

"What about Callox?" Nabelle asked.

"I pray you will forgive me, and refrain from asking me to answer that." Micheel knew she would never forgive him if he told her his plan. "Go and return to the place where we first met, all those years ago, *ya kamar*. I'll be waiting for you."

A portal opened up behind the bed, and Nabelle and Pasher disappeared through it, heading toward their emergency transport. Micheel knew they would be safe, but as soon as they were gone, he felt as though he was gone, too.

Callox started crying, and Micheel longed for the freedom to weep with his son.

"Now I must save you," he told his son. "And unfortunately, that means there are many more tears ahead of us." He carefully placed Callox on the operating table and reached for his scalpel, calling in the required information for the coming surgery.

"I'm so sorry for this, Callox, but Daddy has to amputate that arm."

C. S. JOHNSON

TO BE CONTINUED …

C. S. JOHNSON

THE
BIRTH
OF
GEMINI

°☼°

MANGA VERSION

Story by
C. S. Johnson

Illustrations by
Alkinz

C. S. JOHNSON

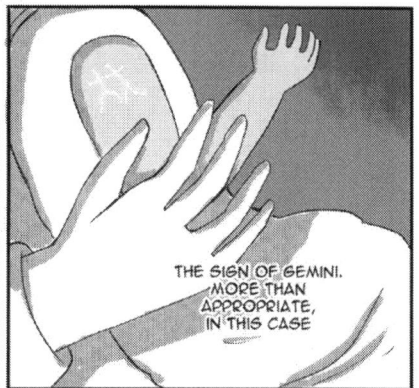

11

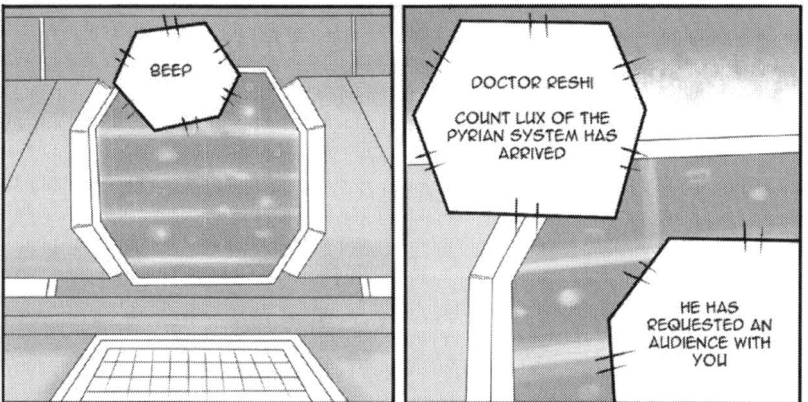

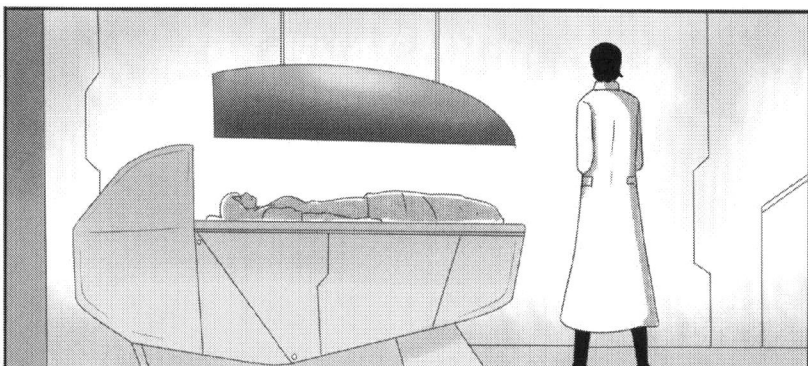

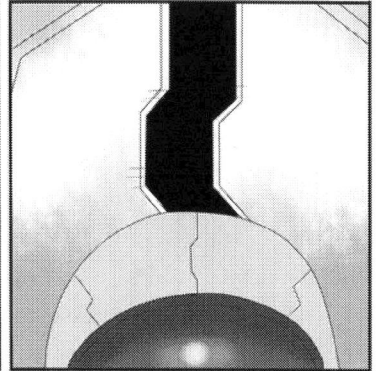

TO BE CONTINUED …

C. S. Johnson is the author of several young adult sci-fi and fantasy novels, including *The Starlight Chronicles* series, the *Once Upon a Princess* saga, and the *Divine Space Pirates* trilogy. With a gift for sarcasm and an apologetic heart, she currently lives in Atlanta with her family.

Please read on for a sample of *The Heights of Perdition*, the first book in The Divine Space Pirates Trilogy, a science fiction romance series from C. S. Johnson.

In an apocalyptic future, Aerie St. Cloud and Exton Shepherd were on opposing sides. But after their accidental encounter, their lives—and the lives of their friends, family, and nations—will never be the same.

C. S. JOHNSON

Chapter 1 from

THE HEIGHTS

OF

PERDITION

BOOK ONE OF *THE DIVINE SPACE PIRATES*

◆◆◆◆

C. S. Johnson

C. S. JOHNSON

♦1♦

At just the right angle, the dark blue and white orb, suspended in a sea of invisible shadows, held in place by a faith as impossible to believe in as it was to see, fit nicely between his fingers. Outside his window, Earth looked small and fragile, seemingly innocent, and mostly harmless. A hollowness slipped between his thumb and forefinger as he squashed them together, crushing the blueberry-sized circle.

Amused by the irony of the forced perspective before him, a rare, genuine smile formed on Exton Shepherd's face.

It was, he decided, almost a shame no one else was around to witness such an unusual event. He smooshed his fingers together, imagining the world completely decimated into dust.

But then, he recalled, he'd given plenty of smiles earlier, as all the hubbub went on about the ship. Surely the crew, his hodgepodge of adopted family and coworkers, would have been satisfied with those, even though they were inauthentic at best and mocking at worst.

Duty sometimes demanded playing happy. Exton knew that, and he followed it, even in instances he loathed.

Like today.

Between the thirteenth and fifteenth sunrises of his day, he'd watched the only other person he truly cared for in all the world—no, he mentally corrected himself, in all the universe—pledge her love, heart, and life to another man.

It was heartbreaking on some levels, but strangely freeing, too.

The wedding had been quaint, warm, and sweet. Its simplicity suggested nothing of its socially taxing nature.

Exton had no regrets about ducking out as soon as the bride and groom finished their vows and the Ecclesia had pronounced them husband and wife.

Once he had successfully slipped out of sight, Exton proceeded to the Captain's Lounge, the small room he'd claimed as his the day after launching the *Perdition* into space. There was little to be said of the room's comfort; it was more like a tall elevator shaft than a room, empty of everything but the coldness of space and a small window hidden up near the far end. More than once, Exton wondered if he'd found a kind of kinship with it; hollow and bleak, with a tiny view looking out toward the fleeing horizon.

It was there, on a window seat built into the windowpane, where Exton tucked his legs under his chin and entered into his own world of privacy, where he was free to be who he wanted, even if it was for only a moment.

As captain of the ship, he didn't want his crew to see him in one of his more melancholy moods.

His frown returned when he opened his fingers again, only to see Earth was still hanging in space before him, its silence mocking and spiteful. Rearranging his hand, he made it seem like he was carrying the earth in the palm. Fleetingly, he toyed with the idea of pretending to toss the small pearl away into the dark recesses of space, into an imaginary hell.

But he knew that would not work.

Exton knew two things with startling clarity and unshakable certainty: The first was that hell was real, and the second was that it was his home.

"Having fun?" a voice asked from below him.

"Huh?" Exton jerked around in surprise, nearly falling off the window ledge. "Come on, Emery, don't do that," he groaned, while the young woman dressed all in white only laughed. His balance, already compromised by the pull of the starship's gravity, faltered again as Exton tried to adjust himself. "You know I don't like it when people interrupt me, especially when I'm here."

"But it's my wedding day," Emery insisted. "And I'd like to have a dance with the ship's captain before the night shift starts. Come on, we're up first."

Exton gave up on staying by the window and jumped down as gracefully as he could. "All the shifts up here are technically the night shift," he grumbled.

"Some would say we live in perpetual day up here on the *Perdition*," Emery offered, her voice gentle even as she maintained her stance. "Sunrise and sunset are only ninety-two minutes apart for us now, when we're this close to Earth."

"Sunrises and sunsets do not make day and night up here," Exton told her, touching his forehead.

Emery reached out and took his hand, before she placed it over his heart. "I think your problem is too much night in here, not out there." She turned her attention back to the window, where six inches of steel-grade glass separated them from the vacuum of space.

Exton followed her gaze, wondering if she was looking for any sign of familiarity from their old home. He watched as the end of the ocean braced itself against the shore of the Old Republic; he felt his memory pull him in, and he could see it clearly inside his mind.

The chill of the old mountains where he would go work and play with his father, the spray of the salt water on his transport module, the warmth of his mother's arms as she welcomed him home from school—all of it embraced him, surrounding him and penetrating into the deep recesses of his heart.

And then there was pain, and then it was gone.

Exton shook his head. "I know it seems like a long time has passed, but it's time to cause the URS some trouble. It's almost the anniversary, you know."

"I know," she replied. A sudden sadness appeared in her gaze, and Exton wondered if she had been reminiscing as well.

Pushing aside his grief, he straightened his shoulders. "I have a plan that will really make them sorry this year, Em."

"I know you're a man of your word," Emery replied, "but I'm not sure it will be enough to convince them to give us what we want."

"They already cannot give us what we want." Exton shrugged. "Our game was never for power. It was for meaning."

"It's not a game, Exton."

"I know it's not!" Out of the corner of his eye, he saw Emery flinch. "I know it's not," he repeated carefully, reverting to his usual, detached tone. "It's not our fault that it became a quest for survival, Emery. I know that even more than you do."

"If it's survival you want," Emery scoffed, "there's no point in selling your soul in the process."

Before Exton could assure Emery he had no soul left that was worth saving, let alone selling, he stopped. Happy times, he reminded himself.

Emery's wedding was a special occasion, one that had excited her for the past several months, offering a glimmer of hope on a horizon of gloom and turmoil. Exton was determined not to let the past rob him—or her—of anything else, so long as it was in his power. "You're right," he acquiesced, momentarily giving in.

Emery smiled brightly, and Exton suddenly had a hard time believing she was only two years younger than he was. At twenty-two, she seemed much more innocent than the figure that gazed back at him when he looked in the mirror.

He slipped his hand out from under hers, before taking and squeezing it. "Are you sure you wouldn't like to have the first dance with your new husband?"

"Tyler is my heart's desire," Emery told him firmly, "but you will always be my hero."

Exton grimaced. He knew he was no hero. "It would be a shame to waste your time with me."

"Time with you is not a waste."

"Did Tyler approve of changing up the dancing order? The man might be in love, but there's no need to make him prove to be the fool."

"Hey, Tyler's your commander, and your best friend," Emery objected. "You know he's not a fool."

"Not where it concerns you. He would be smart to correct that, and I have been telling him since he received approval from the Ecclesia to start courting you," Exton told her. He gave her a devious look. "Should I make him walk the plank?"

Emery frowned and searched the darkened shadows of his face. "That's not funny, Exton."

"I know."

They walked in silence for a few moments before Exton spoke once more. "I don't want to dance. No offense, Em."

"Traditionally, it was the daughter's duty to dance with her father, first." Emery smiled. "But that's more of a cultural thing I've read about from the Old Republic."

"Yes, I remember that," Exton agreed. "Ironic, how the Revolutionary States would be appalled by it now."

Of course, he recalled, even the idea of using the term "father" might have some of the more militant protestors up in arms, as the beloved Daddy Dictator of the URS, Grant Osgood, did not encourage familial relationships, unless such feelings were directed toward government.

"If the URS is against it, you should be more inclined to appease me, then," Emery contended.

There was a breath of silence and stillness before Exton responded. "I'm not our father," he scoffed.

"You're more like him than you might wish."

As Exton scowled at her, Emery pointed her finger at him accusingly. "See? You even have the same exasperated look he used to get when he was frustrated."

"I'll have to take your word for it." Exton shrugged, scratching his head. He frowned as he realized it had been some time since he'd gotten a haircut. His father used to do the same thing, especially when he was planning his next engineering endeavor. Exton suddenly wondered if it was his own scruffy locks that had been making him shrink back from mirrors of late.

He missed his father too much to want to see him staring out of the mirror from the other side of the grave.

Emery chuckled again, drawing him out of his thoughts. "Well, I know at least one trait you share with him. He had a hard time telling me no to anything I wanted, if memory serves."

"You look too much like Mom for me to say no," Exton admitted. "I'm sure he had the same problem, but that's one I'm more willing to share with him."

With her dark brown hair, blue-green eyes, and petite form, Emery was the living memory of their mother. She even had the same dimple hovering above the left corner of her lips, a trait Exton knew was the extent of their common features. Their father's blue eyes, as clear and sharp as ice, had passed to him, along with his height, broad shoulders, and black hair.

"He always did want me to follow in his footsteps," Exton muttered as they headed out of the Captain's Lounge. "But I'm not sure he would have enjoyed the ghost of Captain Chainsword, the infamous space lumberjack pirate."

"I don't think he would have liked it, given how much he derided you for enjoying those fantasy adventures you used to read."

"It seemed fitting at the time, to create a new role for him to play, along with the rest of us."

"I suppose." Emery shrugged. "But Papa was a brilliant engineer, same as you, and a good man. I'm not sure he would have liked your emphasis on piracy and power."

"For the most part, I think you are right," Exton agreed. "But he was too idealistic by far. That was what got him killed." He looked out a nearby window, where, even as he could no longer see Earth, he still felt the pull of its shadow.

"In hindsight, you would prove to be correct on that point."

"That is why I will not make the same mistake as he did. While *Paradise* is out of reach, *Perdition* will do what it can to ensure a better life for us."

"And others, too," Emery added proudly.

"Maybe." Exton shrugged. "I only have a duty to you, and you're technically Tyler's problem now. Anyone else is just extra."

"Your duty to me hasn't ended."

Exton rolled his eyes. "I'm going to dance with you, aren't I? What else is there?"

"Your duty to me might include a dance tonight, but I wish for you to find someone you would love as I love Tyler." She smiled. "Someone you can spend your life trying to make happy."

"Even as life makes me miserable?"

Emery frowned and sighed. "I don't know why you do that."

"Do what?"

"Make it impossible for yourself to be happy."

"Happiness is fleeting, remember?" Exton rolled his eyes. "Even the leaders of the Ecclesia would agree with me there."

"They don't often agree with you, especially when it comes to your mandates," Emery concurred. "The only reason they would on this account is because the phrasing is vague enough to seem to agree on the meaning." She narrowed her gaze. "And the practice."

Exton wrinkled his nose. "We've been up here for too long if you know me so well."

"I still prefer this to when we were off at different universities, working on our studies," Emery admitted with a thoughtful smile. "But as for the argument, you don't seem to agree with the Ecclesia a whole lot, either. You don't share most of their beliefs. I find it hard to believe that you would try to garner support from among their teachings."

"Their teachings on wisdom and life, and how it should be, I respect. But it's different when you're trying to manage a pirate starship and ruin an empire."

"Not to mention when you insist so stubbornly on remaining miserable."

"I *am* going back to your wedding celebration, aren't I?" Exton groaned. "Please don't push it, Em. You know how I feel. If God would grant your wish for me, if he wanted so much for me to be 'happy,' he could have let me 'fall in love' with someone on the *Perdition*, like you and Tyler. But even when we send our smaller ships down to Earth for supplies, see Aunt Patty, or attack the URS, there's no one there for me. There are only people there who want the protection *Perdition* can offer to political dissents or refugees such as themselves."

After a moment of thought, he added, "Besides, my job is to protect and lead aboard the spaceship. The last thing I need is to be led around by the whims of a woman."

"There's no need to make it sound so deplorable," Emery scoffed, arching an eyebrow at him. "Do you honestly think dealing with the moods of a man are any easier?"

He flashed her a charming grin.

"You don't need to set yourself up for failure like that. We have only been up in space for six years now, hiding in the shadows of all the toxic clouds while playing war games with the URS."

"Not to mention watching destruction of all other sorts go unchecked," Exton added, his voice grim.

"It's not all 'unchecked,'" Emery reminded him. "Exton, you still can't lose hope. God is a supposed to be a god of miracles, remember? We have time."

Exton wondered how his sister could be worried about his heart, when his life, as well all the lives of his crew, faced the bigger risk. It was one thing to be aware of danger, but another to disregard it, especially for something as silly as true love.

He studied Emery's daydreaming smile in silence and decided he had the right of it: As much as she was ever his practical and precise sister, Emery's wedded bliss was affecting her judgment.

Exton was surprised at the sudden stab of jealousy. He squashed it down as he caught sight of the approaching Earth through the galley windows.

Didn't Emery see the coming battle? Exton wondered. *Didn't she feel the haunted air about the starship, with specters of the past lurking around every corner of the* Perdition?

They couldn't outlast the URS forever up in space. While Exton and the Ecclesia had established the *Perdition* as a safe haven over the past few years, it was only a matter of time before the URS would come for them, and he knew it would not be to make peace.

"What is it, Exton?" Emery asked, jolting him out of his gloomy thoughts.

Exton sighed. "It's not like God's just going to dump someone into the ship just for me. You might as well save your breath for dancing, Em."

C. S. JOHNSON

Thank you for reading! Please leave a review for this book and check out www.csjohnson.me for other books and updates!

C. S. JOHNSON

Made in the USA
Las Vegas, NV
07 November 2024

11218810R00024